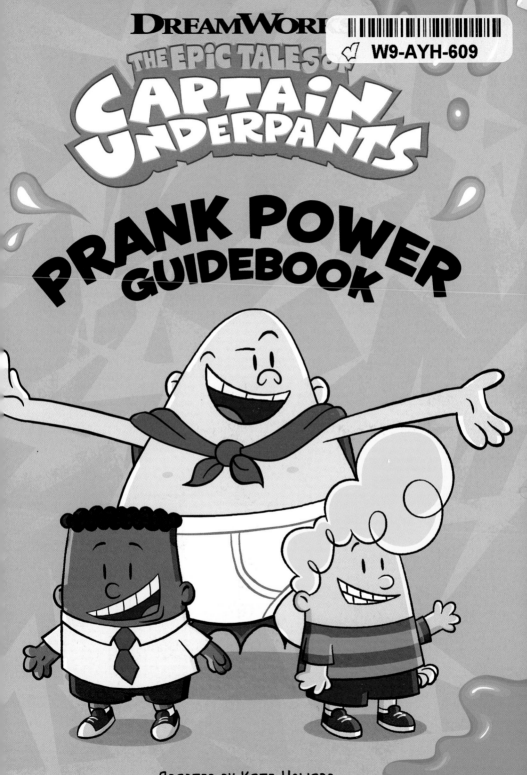

DREAMWORKS

THE EPIC TALES OF CAPTAIN UNDERPANTS

PRANK POWER GUIDEBOOK

ADAPTED BY KATE HOWARD

SCHOLASTIC INC.

W9-AYH-609

© 2019 DreamWorks Animation LLC. All Rights Reserved.

All rights reserved. Published by Scholastic Inc., *Publishers since 1920*. scholastic and associated logos are trademarks and/or registered trademarks of Scholastic Inc. captain underpants, tree house comix, and related designs are trademarks and/or registered trademarks of Dav Pilkey.

"The Captain Underpants Theme Song" written by Jason Gleed (SOCAN), Jordan Yeager (ASCAP), and Peter Hastings (BMI), from the television program *The Epic Tales of Captain Underpants*. Song lyrics used with permission.

The publisher does not have any control over and does not assume any responsibility for author or third-party websites or their content.

No part of this publication may be reproduced, stored in a retrieval system, or transmitted in any form or by any means, electronic, mechanical, photocopying, recording, or otherwise, without written permission of the publisher. For information regarding permission, write to Scholastic Inc., Attention: Permissions Department, 557 Broadway, New York, NY 10012.

This book is a work of fiction. Names, characters, places, and incidents are either the product of the author's imagination or are used fictitiously, and any resemblance to actual persons, living or dead, business establishments, events, or locales is entirely coincidental.

Photos ©: 20-21 background and throughout: vectorplus/Shutterstock.

ISBN 978-1-338-35535-2

10 9 8 7 6 5 4 3 2 1   19 20 21 22 23

Printed in the U.S.A.   40

First printing 2019

Book design by Erin McMahon

CONTENTS

THIS IS GEORGE BEARD AND HAROLD HUTCHINS, AND *I'M* RAP TALKWELL, YOUR HOST HERE ON *CHATTIN' PANTS*. WE'RE HERE TODAY TO CHAT ABOUT THE LATEST ADVENTURES OF CAPTAIN UNDERPANTS!
LAST TIME WE CHECKED IN WITH GEORGE AND HAROLD, THERE WAS A LOT GOING ON IN PIQUA! LET'S TAKE A LOOK AT SOME HIGHLIGHTS OF THE CAPTAIN'S ADVENTURES . . .

But the big, breaking news coming out of Jerome Horwitz Elementary is:
EXPELLED
George and Harold were recently EXPELLED!
Principal Krupp got FIRED!

AND GROWN-UP MELVINBORG HAS TRAVELED BACK IN TIME FROM THE FUTURE . . .

... TO TAKE OVER THE SCHOOL!

GEORGE & HAROLD

In case you weren't paying attention in class, here's a quick re-introduction to some of the key players in this Piqua-drama.

First up, we've got George Beard. He's the kid on the left with the tie and the flat top.

Harold is the one on the right with the t-shirt and the bad haircut. Remember that, now.

George and Harold are best friends and fourth graders at Jerome Horwitz Elementary. They're also fairly well known as some of the biggest pranksters to ever set foot at this school.

SOME OF THEIR MOST LEGENDARY PRANKS INCLUDE:

REPLACING TOILET PAPER WITH SANDPAPER

GLUE-FROSTED COOKIES

SKUNK SPRAY IN THE AIR VENTS!

TREE HOUSE COMIX

George and Harold are also the brains behind the world-famous (okay . . . maybe more like *Piqua*-famous) Tree House Comix, Inc. Inside their backyard tree house headquarters, these two have created some of the most amazing comic superheroes and villains ever.

16

CH-CH-CH-CHANGES

Now, remember how we just told you these two pranksters got expelled from Jerome Horwitz Elementary? And how *Melvin* and future *Melvinborg* have taken over the school, stepping in as principal after Mr. Krupp got fired?

Thanks to some quick thinking (and Grace Wain, a smarty-pants new superintendent), George and Harold found a *loophole* and were able to go back to school.

GRACE WAIN

MR. KRUPP'S HANDWRITTEN RULES AREN'T OFFICIAL RULES, SO THE EXPULSION OF GEORGE BEARD AND HAROLD HUTCHINS IS REPEALED!

Fine. If George and Harold are back, they're back. But Grace Wain can't stop me from Melvinizing the school!

Mwahaha!

YES, THAT'S RIGHT. WITH MELVIN AND PRINCIPAL MELVINBORG IN CHARGE, EVERYTHING WAS COMPLETELY DIFFERENT AT SCHOOL.

GEORGE AND HAROLD QUICKLY REALIZED THEY WERE LIVING IN THE WORST KIND OF NIGHTMARE: A NIGHTMARE THAT WAS *REAL*. THE SCHOOL HAD GOTTEN A MELVIN MAKEOVER. IT WAS MELVIN *EVERYWHERE*, ALL THE TIME. HIS IMAGE WAS ON THE WALLS AND CEILINGS, GIANT MELVIN BALLOONS HOVERED OVER THE PLAYGROUND, AND EVEN THE *BATHROOM STALLS* HAD BEEN MELVINIZED!

Unfortunately, George and Harold had no choice but to figure out how to deal with Melvin and, uh . . . the other Melvin. Because this year, they had a lot on the line: If they made it through the year without getting into any major trouble, their parents had *finally* agreed to let them go to Lake Summer Camp.

LAKE SUMMER CAMP:
The opposite of school.

SWIMMING!

S'MORES!

FUN!

(TO MAKE A LONG STORY SHORT: THEY GO. BUT BEFORE WE CAN TELL YOU THAT STORY, WE HAVE TO TELL YOU *THIS* STORY . . .)

As you probably already know, Melvin is *obsessed* with his grades—and how much better he is than everyone else. So, when they take over, he and Principal Melvinborg introduce a new feature at school . . .

IF THEY WANT TO GO TO SUMMER CAMP, GEORGE AND HAROLD HAVE TO GET *ABOVE* THE PASSING LINE. SO, THEY'RE PUTTING ALL THEIR EFFORT INTO EARNING EXTRA CREDIT TO BOOST THEIR GRADES!

IF THEY DON'T FINISH THE YEAR WITH AT LEAST A C AVERAGE, **NO CAMP.**

Melvin's still number one. And we keep sinking farther and farther below the good grades line.

RANK TANK 2000

MELVIN
ERICA
EMILY
IVAN
MADDIE
CHRIS
GOOCH
JOSE
SEAN
DRESSY
ASHLEY
SAM
HEATHER
JOEL
KARL
MARTIN
ANDREW
SUE
GEORGE
HAROLD
PAUL
RYAN
BECCA
POLLY
PENELOPE
DEMI

MR. KRUPP

Remember this guy? It's Mr. Krupp, the principal everyone loves to hate!

YOU'RE TRESPASSING! I'M GOING TO HAVE YOU ALL ARRESTED!

VISITS
4 2 3

After getting fired, Mr. Krupp tried to create a life outside the walls of Jerome Horwitz Elementary. But he wasn't quite sure what to do with himself. He quickly discovered that not being a principal was difficult and confusing.

I'VE CALLED YOU HERE BECAUSE I'M THE PRINCIPAL OF THIS SCHOOL, AND I'VE HAD IT WITH YOUR SHENANIGANS!

FUN FACT: Mr. Krupp's favorite food is guacamole!

Surprisingly, George and Harold kind of missed having crabby ol' Krupp around (especially when the alternative was the Melvins!). So, they helped get Mr. Krupp back to school. But when he returned, it was in a whole new role . . . *VICE* principal.

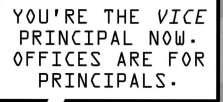

YOU'RE THE *VICE* PRINCIPAL NOW. OFFICES ARE FOR PRINCIPALS.

KRUPP'S NEW DIGS:

BEING THE MELVINS' LOWLY ASSISTANT MEANS MR. KRUPP HAS TO PERFORM ALL KINDS OF AWFUL JOBS. LIKE THE TIME HE HAD TO DRESS UP AS A KID TO TRY TO FIND OUT WHAT GEORGE AND HAROLD WERE UP TO . . . AND MAKE SURE THEY WOULDN'T SUCCEED!

CAPTAIN UNDERPANTS

The only thing that *hasn't* changed for Mr. Krupp is his secret identity as **CAPTAIN UNDERPANTS**.

When things get out of hand in Piqua, George and Harold can snap their fingers and grumpy old Mr. Krupp turns into everyone's favorite crime-fighting superhero!

This tighty-whitey clad hero battles bad guys, saving Piqua one comic foe at a time.

CAPTAIN UNDERPANTS SUPA-RECAP:
The Origin of Captain Underpants
(theme song edition!)

So, George and Harold make comic books . . .

We're cool.

Me, too!

FLIP-O-RAMA™!

STEP 1: PLACE YOUR LEFT HAND ON THE DOTTED LINES WHERE IT SAYS "LEFT HAND HERE." HOLD THE BOOK FLAT.

STEP 2: HOLD THE CORNER OF THE RIGHT-HAND PAGE WITH YOUR THUMB AND INDEX FINGER.

STEP 3: NOW QUICKLY FLIP THE RIGHT PAGE BACK AND FORTH UNTIL THE PICTURES LOOK LIKE THEY'RE MOVING. FOR EXTRA FUN, DON'T FORGET TO ADD YOUR OWN SOUND EFFECTS.

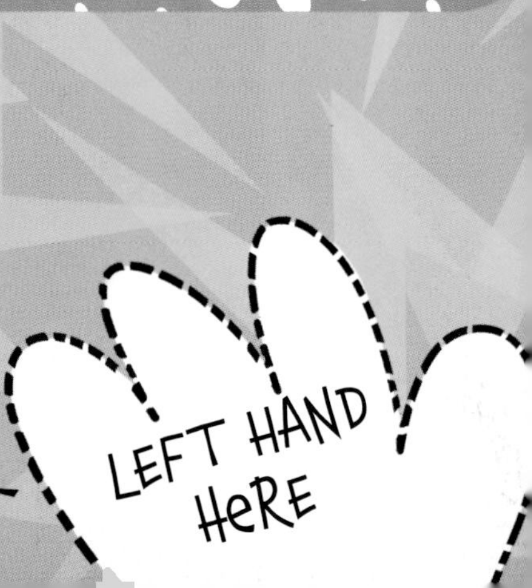

32

LEFT HAND HERE

RIGHT
THUMB
HERE

MELVIN SNEEDLY ELEMENTARY

While this may look like Jerome Horwitz Elementary, this school is now called **MELVIN SNEEDLY ELEMENTARY!**

MELVIN SNEEDLY ELEMENTARY

SNOOTY LATIN MOTTO COMING SOON!

MELVIN SNEEDLY E

IT'S NOW COOL TO TOOT

WITH THE MELVINS IN CHARGE, THERE WERE A LOT OF CHANGES IN STORE FOR THE SCHOOL FORMERLY KNOWN AS JEROME HORWITZ ELEMENTARY. MELVIN HAD ONE MAJOR GOAL IN LIFE: TO GET INTO THE PRESTIGIOUS AND CHALLENGING ELITEANATI ACADEMY. TO DO *THAT*, HE HAD TO FINISH THE YEAR TOP IN HIS CLASS—AND PROVE HE WAS EXACTLY THE KIND OF

TO PREPARE MY CHILDHOOD SELF FOR ELITEANATI ACADEMY, I'LL TURN THIS INTO THE SMARTEST, MOST SUPERIOR ELEMENTARY SCHOOL ANYWHERE!

STUDENT ELITEANATI WAS LOOKING FOR!

THE MELVINS EVEN BUILT A DETENTION DUNGEON TO KEEP TROUBLEMAKERS (LIKE GEORGE AND HAROLD) IN LINE!

Hey, buddy. It's us again . . .

ONCE WE'VE TURNED THIS SCHOOL INTO A WORLD-CLASS INSTITUTION OF LEARNING, ELITEANATI ACADEMY WILL BE BEGGING FOR YOU, ITS STAR STUDENT, TO ATTEND!

Eliteanati Academy

MELVIN SNEEDLY

So what, exactly, makes Melvin Sneedly so special? His brains and his inventions!

Extra work is my specialty. But then, what isn't? I'm great.

I excavated this sample from **Piqua** Glacier. When I thaw it with my *ThawAndOrder 2000*, I'll have an actual dinosaur!

THE YouChooseYouFuse 2000:

USED TO FUSE ANY TWO CREATURES TOGETHER INTO ONE MAGNIFICENT AND ALL-POWERFUL BEAST!

Krupp was bad, but at least when he was here we didn't have to learn. I can't believe I'm saying this, but... I miss Krupp!

(TO MAKE A LONG STORY SHORT: KRUPP COMES BACK. BUT WE ALREADY TOLD YOU THAT.)

EVEN THOUGH MELVIN WOULD LIKE TO BELIEVE HE'S THE ONLY STUDENT WHO MATTERS AT JEROME HORWITZ ... UH, *MELVIN SNEEDLY* ELEMENTARY ... HE'S NOT. THERE ARE PLENTY OF OTHER CHARACTERS THAT HELP GEORGE AND HAROLD PLAY OUT THEIR CLEVER SCHEMES AND GET INTO TROUBLE OF THEIR VERY OWN.

ERICA WANG: Prank aficionado and all-around smart kid

After Erica helped George and Harold write a comic about an evil toilet clog, Erica makes her debut as Captain Underpants's sidekick, **PLUNGERINA**!

The rain forest is our planet's greatest treasure!

DRESSY KILLMAN: The Dreamer

This music-loving free spirit is always up for adventure . . . and happily joins George and Harold's quest to search for Mr. Krupp in the jungle of Ecuador.

By chipping away at the clay, your sculpture begins to take form.

BO HWEEMUTH: The Artist

Kindhearted Bo is best known for his amazing clay art—and became friends with George and Harold after creating custom sculptures of some of their best-known superheroes and villains.

JESSICA GORDON & THE SOPHIES:
The Girl with Beautiful Hair . . . and Her Minions

JESSICA GORDON IS A TOTAL DRAMA QUEEN WHO LOVES BEING THE CENTER OF ATTENTION. SHE EXPECTS THE SOPHIES TO WAIT ON HER HAND AND FOOT AT ALL TIMES.

AFTER AN UNFORTUNATE MIX-UP, OTHER SOPHIE AND A TREE SLOTH SWAP PLACES IN THE JUNGLES OF ECUADOR ON THE GANG'S TRIP TO TRY TO FIND MR. KRUPP (MORE ON THAT LATER). EVEN *MORE* UNFORTUNATELY, NO ONE EVEN REALIZED THAT THEIR CLASSMATE HAD BEEN REPLACED BY A SLOTH.

FUN FACT: While in the jungle, the *real* Other Sophie gets taken prisoner by the croc-o-bats!

Sophie One, you're doing a great job. Other Sophie, you're brushing like an animal.

THE TEACHERS
AT MELVIN SNEEDLY ELEMENTARY

MR. MEANER: GYM

IN NEED OF A FRESH NEW SUPERHERO WHILE MR. KRUPP IS GONE, GEORGE AND HAROLD PICKED THE NEXT BEST TEACHER CANDIDATE AND TURNED HIM INTO **SERGEANT BOXERS**!

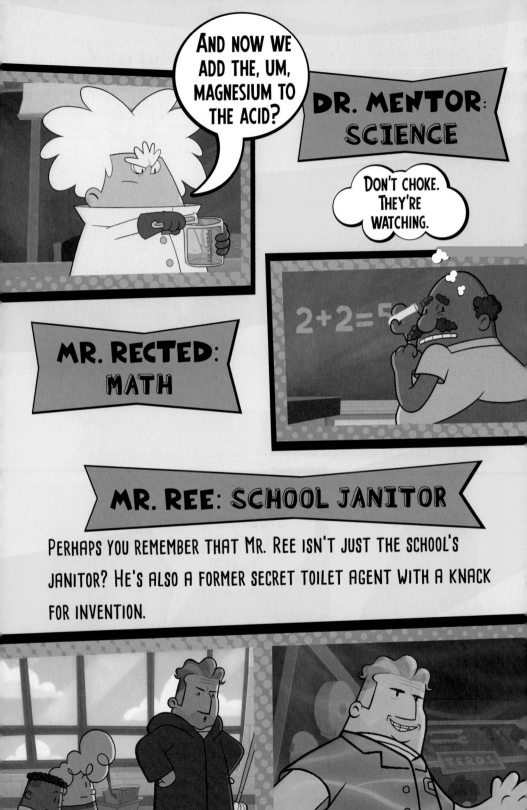

MR. FYDE: A TREE

UNFORTUNATELY, FORMER TEACHER
MR. FYDE HASN'T BEEN AROUND
MUCH . . . EVER SINCE GEORGE AND
HAROLD ACCIDENTALLY TURNED HIM
INTO A GIANT, ANGRY, WALKING
AVOCADO PIT WHO FELL INTO A HOLE
AND GREW INTO AN AVOCADO TREE.
BUT THAT'S A WHOLE 'NOTHER
STORY.

TREE HOUSE COMIX, INC.

PROUDLY PRESENTS:

THE ADVENTURES OF CAPTAIN UNDERPANTS

NOW LET'S GET INTO SOME OF THE LATEST ACTION . . .

After Melvin and future Melvinborg replaced all the teachers at school with robots, George and Harold decided it was time to take matters into their own hands. They had to take down the evil Teachertrons. But without Principal Krupp at school, Captain Underpants wasn't around to help. Time for a new hero . . . and a comic to help teach him what to do!

One time these mean robots kicked all of the teachers out and took over the school.

They were like, "BEEP! BORP! We are robots! We don't like humans."

"Now do math!"

It was a real drag because math is boring and because robots are mean and hate dance music.

Then a robot bonked him on the head and he went asleep and was all HONK SHOE HONK SHOE BURP!

Later, Sergeant Boxers woke up with his wallet missing.

He was all, "This is a problem. I gotta learn how to hero!"

So, he called the Hero Helpline.

Guess who answered? Captain Underpants!

They worked the heavy bag and walked on hot coals and Sergeant Boxers was all:

I GET IT. PRETTY MUCH.

BANG!

So, Sergeant Boxers took his boxer bazooka and boxer-blasted those bots to Bakersfield.

And he was finally a hero. Okay, the end.

HeRo GRaduate

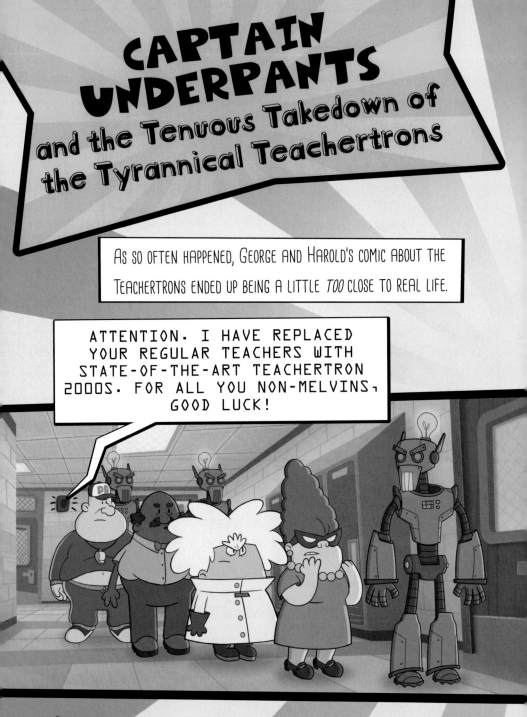

NOW THAT THE MELVINS WERE GROWING EVEN MORE POWER-HUNGRY, GEORGE AND HAROLD DECIDED THEY NEEDED TO FIND MR. KRUPP AND BRING HIM BACK TO SCHOOL . . . BUT TO DO THAT, THEY WERE GONNA NEED SOME HELP. SO, THEY WROTE A SPECIAL ISSUE OF CAPTAIN UNDERPANTS TO CONVINCE THEIR CLASSMATES TO JOIN THEM AS A TEAM OF M.I.S.F.A.R.T.S. (THE MEGA! INCREDIBLE! SEARCH! FORCE! ACTION! RESCUE! TEAM! SQUAD!).

So, this principal booked a trip to the jungle because he loved pythons and, like, malaria.

But when he got there, monkeys stole his map. Cuz, monkeys.

Then the principal fell down a cliff and into a river of piranhas and over a waterfall . . .

And onto a parrot party and through a bunch of lemurs . . .

The signal reached the M.I.S.F.A.R.T.S.!

There was Thinks, the smart one. Thumps, the strong one. Winks, the grizzled vet. And Codes, the gizmo one. (There were some other ones, too, but they were in the bathroom.)

THINKS
THUMPS
WINKS
CODES

Thinks made a plan. The M.I.S.F.A.R.T.S. flew to the jungle in a hover-jet-tank-bus-scooter-rocket.

Then Codes located the lost guys with a laser lost-guy-finder he built.

And Thumps jumped into the volcano . . .

. . . and punched the lava-gators.

Codes cooled the lava with a laser lava-cooler thingy he built.

And the M.I.S.F.A.R.T.S. rescued the principal and Captain Underpants from the volcano.

Cuz they were a team of cool kids who did this impossible thing cuz they were a team and cool. Don't you wish you could be one? Yeah!

CAPTAIN UNDERPANTS
and the Frantic Fury of the Fearsome Furculees

After George and Harold learned that Mr. Krupp was in Ecuador searching for the magical Fountain of Hair . . .

Fountain of Hair

They put together a group of M.I.S.F.A.R.T.S. that could help them find Krupp and bring him home.

As always, things didn't go *quite* as planned. They found Mr. Krupp, but then the real Furculees came after them . . .

I am **Furculees**, guardian of the **Fountain of Hair! This** bad hair day will be your worst!

It was time to snap Captain Underpants into action to defeat the furry beast and get all the M.I.S.F.A.R.T.S. back home safely!

HAIR-O-RA-MAAAAAAAAAAA!

Now that Krupp was back in Piqua, George and Harold hoped things would get back to normal. But alas: no such luck. Melvin and Principal Melvinborg were just as power-hungry as always, and they had no intention of turning over their school to Mr. Krupp. Instead, they turned all the teachers at school into bees. Total **BUZZ**KILL. So George and Harold wrote another comic to try to figure out how to get out of this sticky situation.

So, once there was this teacher named Ms. Beegotten, who had a beehive hairdo, which really just looked like a cotton candy stuck to her head.

Ms. Beegotten's hairdo started attracting killer bees.

They moved in, put up a "Hair is where the home is" sign over their door . . .

. . . and threw a hair-warming party (which sounds like a salon treatment, but it's not).

But Captain Underpants super-loved honey, so he ate it all . . .

. . . and got crazy-big. Fat-dinosaur big! (No offense to dinosaurs.)

But Captain Underpants didn't become a zombee with two e's, because . . .

SUPER TUM-TUM!

Anyway, Captain Underpants tried to fly away, but he was over his maximum launch weight.

So, he fell on Queen Zombee instead, and she was trapped under his big fat butt forever . . . or until he burned off all those calories with spinning classes and low carbs.

CAPTAIN UNDERPANTS
and the Harmful Horrors of the Harrowing Hiveschool

When the Melvins injected all the teachers at school with bee DNA . . .

. . . using their new Bee-N-A-In-U 2000 . . .

. . . they planned to become the King Bee and control the teachers using Principal Melvinborg's hive mind controller!

BUT THEN MS. RIBBLE ACCIDENTALLY BECAME THE QUEEN BEE INSTEAD. AND SHE COULD CONTROL ALL THE OTHER TEACHERS WITH A BUTT WIGGLE. (YEAH, THINGS GOT WEIRD.)
GEORGE AND HAROLD HAD TO FIGURE OUT HOW TO GET THEIR SCHOOL OUT OF A BEE-MERGENCY SITUATION. TIME FOR CAPTAIN UNDERPANTS!
Tra-La-Bees? I'm allergic to bees! I'm ten pounds of me in a five-pound bag!
You mezzed with the wrong beehive. Your fate is zealed!
EVEN THOUGH CAPTAIN UNDERPANTS WAS DOWN FOR THE COUNT AFTER ALL THOSE PESKY BEE STINGS, HE STILL MANAGED TO SAVE THE DAY!
Let's turn him into a BEE-tering ram!

CAPTAIN UNDERPANTS AND THE POOPY POOPACABRA

EVEN WITH MR. KRUPP'S RETURN TO SCHOOL, THINGS WEREN'T IMPROVING MUCH FOR GEORGE AND HAROLD. IN FACT, LAKE SUMMER CAMP WAS LOOKING MORE UNLIKELY THAN EVER! IF THEY DIDN'T GET THEIR GRADES UP SOON, SUMMER CAMP WOULD BE NOTHING MORE THAN A FAR-OFF DREAM.

TO ENTERTAIN THEMSELVES WHILE WORKING ON A TOUGH (AND BORING!) SCHOOL ASSIGNMENT THAT THEY HOPED THEY WOULD ACE, GEORGE AND HAROLD WROTE AN EPIC COMIC ABOUT THE POOPY POOPACABRA.

So, there was this teacher who wanted to get invited to parties . . .

. . . but he didn't cuz he smelled like beans (cuz he always made cheesy bean dip that smelled like beans).

He got all mad and stuff and made a sewage sprayer to ruin the parties.

But when he pressed the button, all the sewage went on him—whoa, wrong way!

Captain Underpants grabbed a lawn gnome and smashed it over Poopacabra's head.

Poopacabra grabbed a pink flamingo and swung it.

But right when he was about to chuck a plastic snowman, Captain Underpants saw a single tear in Poopacabra's eye and he knew . . .

. . . Poopacabra was just a good guy who caught a bad and very smelly break.

CAPTAIN UNDERPANTS
and the Preposterous Pulverizing of the Pestering Poopacabra

Hoping to boost their grades into the passing zone—and earn their ticket to Lake Summer Camp—by turning in an above-average project, George and Harold figured out how to train their science lab rat to do the best trick ever.

We taught him how to draw a comic book!

But after *MELVIN'S* LAB ANIMAL MADE A BATCH OF UNPREDICTABLE GREEN TOXIC SLUDGE THAT GLOWED . . .

. . . AND SOME GOT ON GEORGE AND HAROLD'S RAT, RATRICK, THINGS TOOK A TURN FOR THE WORSE. GOODBYE, RATRICK. HELLO, REAL-LIFE POOPACABRA!

TIME TO CALL ON CAPTAIN UNDERPANTS!

BUT THEN GEORGE AND HAROLD REMEMBERED THAT ONLY A *CHUPACABRA* CAN STOP ANOTHER CHUPACABRA. SO, USING MR. MEANER AS BAIT TO LURE THE LEGENDARY BEAST . . .

. . . THEY CROSSED THEIR FINGERS AND HOPED AN EPIC BATTLE OF **CHUPACABRA** VS. **POOPACABRA** MIGHT SOLVE ALL THEIR PROBLEMS.

RPRISE TWIST! ULTIMATELY, IT WAS **TRUE LOVE** THAT GOT THIS **POOPACABRA** OUT OF PIQUA.

CAPTAIN UNDERPANTS and the JOKEY JOKEaSAURUS

In an attempt to make up for their science project snafu and earn some much-needed extra credit in Ms. Ribble's class, George and Harold wrote a comic book report about dinosaurs . . . starring their brave, bold superhero **CAPTAIN UNDERPANTS!**

(To make a long story short: The comic didn't go over quite as well as they'd been expecting it to. Teachers never appreciate quality work.)

One day, this scientist guy wanted to write a dinosaur book.

So, he went to the time-machine store, rented a time machine, and went back to dinosaur times.

When he got there, it was jungle-y and smelled like eggs.

But the dinosaurs could talk and were like us. They had mini-golf and pizza places and snack bars.

And even bad stuff, like overdue books from the library and junk.

Then the scientist met a dinosaur named Diddly Saurus who loved to prank.

Diddly Saurus knew all the best pranks, like putting mayo in a donut, and hiding all the furniture in the garage.

Captain Underpants pulled out a bunch of undies and tied them into an under-whip.

It was on like a mastodon. Tighty-whitey versus taily-whaley!

Diddly smacked Captain Underpants with his tail, back into the snack bar. And he smashed into the Freezilee Slush Bucket machine.

MMM! CHERRY-ISH!

Then as Diddly got real close, Captain Underpants blasted him with the Freezilee Slush Bucket machine and stopped him cold!

Ice-cold! FREEZILEE!

Ice-cold Diddly slid all the way down a hill and— *SPLASH!*—floated away on a river to nowhere!

CAPTAIN UNDERPANTS
and the Dastardly Deeds of the Devious Diddly Saurus

As usual, life began to imitate art . . . and George and Harold's latest comic suddenly became all-too-real. Instead of earning extra credit, they created a lot of extra trouble instead.

When George and Harold went back in time to the Jurassic Period (using Melvin's Time Toad 2000) . . .

. . . they accidentally dropped a copy of their latest comic in the jungle. It quickly became a magical book of knowledge for dinosaurs, and gave them a bunch of ideas for how to make mischief.

THEN, WHEN DINOSAURS SHOWED UP IN MODERN TIMES AND STARTED TO CREATE TROUBLE AT THE MINI-GOLF PLACE . . .

. . . IT WAS UP TO GEORGE, HAROLD, AND CAPTAIN UNDERPANTS TO GET EVERYONE TO *CHILL* OUT USING SOME OF THE EXACT SAME TRICKS THEY WROTE ABOUT IN THEIR COMIC!

CAPTAIN UNDERPANTS and the SINISTER SPLOTCH

By Beard and Hutchins
Lawyers-at-Law

Attorneys

STILL REELING FROM THE DINO-SIZED PROBLEMS CAUSED BY DIDDLY SAURUS AND FRIENDS, GEORGE AND HAROLD HAD BEGUN TO REALIZE THEY **REALLY** NEEDED TO BUCKLE DOWN AND GET THEIR GRADES UP. AFTER ALL, THEIR TICKET TO SUMMER CAMP WAS ON THE LINE! BUT AFTER AN EVIL IMPOSTER CALLED SPLOTCH PRETENDED TO BE CAPTAIN UNDERPANTS AND WENT ON A STEALING SPREE IN PIQUA, GEORGE AND HAROLD GOT A LITTLE DISTRACTED BY A NEW PROBLEM. TO HELP SOLVE IT, THEY PUT TOGETHER THIS COMIC TO TRY TO PROVE THE REAL CAPTAIN'S INNOCENCE!

One time, there was an evil robe guy named Splotch. (He looked a lot like a certain you-know-who.)

Splotch wanted to take over the world with bathrobes (which doesn't sound like a great plan, but yeah . . .).

So, he pretended to be Captain Underpants, but dark and evil, and he started messin' stuff up.

CAPTAIN UNDERPANTS
and the Shadowy Syndrome
of the Sinister Splotch

AFTER THE NEWS SHOWED FOOTAGE OF A CRIMINAL WHO LOOKED SUSPICIOUSLY LIKE CAPTAIN UNDERPANTS . . .

"SECURITY CAMERAS SHOW THE ROBBER IS A GROWN MAN IN UNDERWEAR AND CAPE. IT'S A VERY SPECIFIC LOOK."

. . . GEORGE AND HAROLD DECIDED TO INVESTIGATE SO THEY COULD GET CAPTAIN UNDERPANTS OUT OF TROUBLE. THEY DISCOVERED AN EVIL **ROBE**—THE VERY *SAME* ROBE THAT GAVE GEORGE AND HAROLD'S OLD PAL JUDGE J.O.R.T.S. HIS SUPERPOWERS ONCE UPON A TIME!—WAS TO BLAME FOR ALL THE TROUBLE IN TOWN.

If you can't prove he's innocent, he'll go to jail forever!

Once I was just a troublemaking alien robe. But Captain Underpants punched me into toxic waste, making me a super robe with his powers!

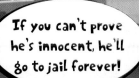

I took over Mr. Ree's body . . .

...and created Bed of Robeses, a dryer sheet that lets me control all robes. Then I framed Captain Underpants for a bunch of crimes to get rid of the only one who could defeat me!

LUCKILY, GEORGE AND HAROLD WERE ABLE TO BREAK CAPTAIN UNDERPANTS OUT OF JAIL JUST IN TIME TO HELP PREVENT...

TOTAL ROBAL DOMINATION!

CAPTAIN UNDERPANTS
& the
CROC-O-BAT BUTT-ERFLY CONUNDRUM BLUNDER

WITH LIFE GOING BACK TO NORMAL AT SCHOOL (OR AS NORMAL AS IT GETS AT MELVIN SNEEDLY ELEMENTARY), IT MEANT THINGS WERE ALSO GOING BACK TO **BORING**. TO LIVEN THINGS UP ON THE PLAYGROUND, GEORGE AND HAROLD USED MELVIN'S YOUCHOOSE-YOUFUSE 2000 TO CREATE AN ARMY OF BUTT-ERFLIES . . . BUT THEN THEY COULDN'T FIGURE OUT HOW TO GET RID OF THEM. WHAT'S THE BEST WAY TO SOLVE ANY PROBLEM? MAKE A COMIC!

Recess is a time for fun. But there was a smart kid who loved science and hated fun. Let's call him Nelvin.

One day, Nelvin built a machine that—*BZATT!*

—made croc-o-bats, which are half-crocodile, half-bat, and all awesome.

But they ruined recess by swooping around with their fangs, so bummer.

Luckily, Captain Underpants was flying by, so he swooped down and he twirled some undies so fast that he opened a wedgie wormhole!

YEE-HAW!

YAY!!

He herded the croc-o-bats into the wedgie wormhole like a croc-o-bat cowboy. (And they went somewhere else far away so, like, don't worry about it.)

And the kids were so happy.

Especially some kids named George and Harold (who may be inspired by actual persons and events). They wanted to celebrate so they borrowed—not stole—Nelvin's machine and they combined butts and flies to make butt-erflies.

And even though the butt-erflies were hilarious—I mean, flying butts, right?

They were also dangerous and crazy.

They chased all the kids. They hid out in the cafeteria, but the butt-erflies ate through the walls like hungry lawn mowers!

But it all worked out fine cuz Captain Underpants stopped the butt-erflies, too!

CAPTAIN UNDERPANTS
and the Bizarre Blitzkrieg of the Bothersome Butt-erflies

AFTER MELVIN USED HIS **YOUCHOOSEYOUFUSE** 2000 TO CREATE CROC-O-BATS (THE ULTIMATE ENFORCER!) TO STOP ALL THE SHENANIGANS (AND FUN) ON THE PLAYGROUND . . .

If you splice the wrong things together, the resulting mutation can be catastrophic!
GEORGE AND HAROLD DECIDED IT REALLY WOULD BE FUN TO COMBINE **BUTTS** AND **FLIES** TO MAKE BUTT-ERFLIES. TO MAKE A LONG STORY SHORT: IT WAS A DISASTER.
I'm here to save your butts from those butts!
Time for us to dance cheek to cheek to cheek to cheek to . . . you get it. I'm shakin' my bacon to victory!
LEFT HAND HERE

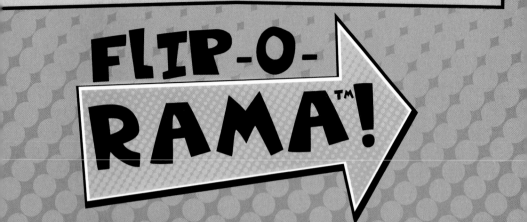

RIGHT
THUMB
HERE

CAPTAIN UNDERPANTS
And the Catastrophic
CLOGGERNAUT
Featuring PLUNGERINA

GEORGE AND HAROLD COULDN'T WAIT TO GET BACK TO WORK ON THEIR LATEST COMIC BOOK.
BUT WHEN IT CAME TIME TO SIT DOWN AND CREATE, THEIR BRAINS WERE TOTALLY **FRIED**
FROM HOMEWORK. (YET THEY **STILL** HADN'T MANAGED TO BOOST THEMSELVES UP AND OVER
THE GOOD GRADES LINE ON MELVIN'S RANK TANK 2000!)

SO ERICA OFFERED TO HELP THEM OUT . . . AND SHE CAME UP WITH AN ALL-NEW SUPERHERO:
PLUNGERINA! AFTERWARD, SHE TRIED TO CONVINCE GEORGE AND HAROLD THAT PLUNGERINA
WAS EVEN **BETTER** THAN CAPTAIN UNDERPANTS. WAS THAT POSSIBLE?

So, once there was a big ball game at the big ball-game stadium.

When the fans went to the bathroom, all the toilets were clogged!

And the fans were like, "We gotta go! It's an emergency!"

AHHHHH!

And a deep voice said:

TOO BAD! MWA-HA-HA!

(Which is bad cuz only evil things put a "Mwa" in front of their "Ha-ha-ha.")

Then a hulky, muscly clog came out of the pipes!

I'M CLOGGERNAUT AND NOTHING CAN STOP ME FROM CLOGGING STUFF!

Then he went on a clogging spree, clogging the field . . .

. . . the peanut guy . . .

. . . and the overpriced souvenir stand where they sell those expensive foam fingers.

Captain Underpants rounded the bases.

HEY, PLUNGERINA, WANNA BE ON MY UNDIE TEAM?

I SUPPOSE.

So, Captain Underpants poured a jug of sports drink on her to celebrate, even though no one likes that, including Plungerina.

WOOMPA—SWACK!

So, she plunge-whacked him.

And then everyone went to the bathroom.

CAPTAIN UNDERPANTS
and the Problematic Pandemonium of the Punishing Plungerina

> All I'm saying is, if Cloggernaut was *real*, Captain Underpants would need **Plungerina** to bail him out.

To try to prove Erica wrong (and demonstrate that Captain Underpants is *far* superior to Plungerina or any other superhero), George and Harold decided to do something that was not very smart: They created an epic clog monster to show that Captain Underpants could handle *anything*.

> I am CLOGGERNAUT!

Enter Mr. Rected, whose afternoon trip to the toilet took a terrifying turn when he turned into Cloggernaut!

With Captain Underpants out of town (at a principal convention, obviously), someone else had to save the day. That's when the boys got a *big* surprise: real-life Plungerina stepped up, ready to flush out the clog!

I'm Plungerina. And you're going down . . . the drain!

But when things got out of hand and Miss Anthrope turned into . . .

. . . it was double the toilet trouble.

Your pipes are about to be cleaned!

It would ultimately take **TWO** superheroes (and a whole lot of flushing) to get rid of *this* clog problem: Captain Underpants *and* Plungerina!

Your puny plungers are no match for my monumental muck!

TOILETASTICS

So, who was the real-life Plungerina? Erica! As it turned out, sometimes Captain Underpants *did* need a little help. George and Harold couldn't help but wonder . . . what would happen if Captain Underpants had a full-time team?

CAPTAIN UNDERPANTS

SECRET WEAPON OF THE STONE FACED KIDS

UNFORTUNATELY, IT LOOKED LIKE GEORGE AND HAROLD WOULD NEVER GET TO FIND OUT WHAT LIFE WOULD BE LIKE IF CAPTAIN UNDERPANTS HAD A TEAM. IN FACT, IT LOOKED LIKE THEY WOULDN'T EVEN HAVE **CAPTAIN UNDERPANTS** AROUND SCHOOL AT ALL ANYMORE! THAT JUST WASN'T ACCEPTABLE. SO WHEN MR. KRUPP ACCEPTED A NEW JOB AS PRINCIPAL AT A **DIFFERENT** SCHOOL, GEORGE AND HAROLD DECIDED TO FOLLOW HIM THERE FOR A CHANGE OF SCENERY. BUT THE KIDS AT THIS SCHOOL NEVER HAD ANY FUN! SO, GEORGE AND HAROLD WROTE A COMIC TO HELP SHAKE THINGS UP.

CAPTAIN UNDERPANTS
and the Bombastic Blathering of the Brainy Blabulous

THIS ONE TIME, GEORGE AND HAROLD DECIDED THEY NEEDED TO ESCAPE FROM THE MELVINS' NEW ANTI-PRANK MEASURES . . .

Herome Jorwitz Elementary? Best School in Quipa?

Those words sound so familiar . . .

. . . AND BE CLOSER TO PRINCIPAL KRUPP. SO, THEY ENROLLED IN A SCHOOL THAT WAS ALMOST *EXACTLY* LIKE JEROME HORWITZ—IF JEROME HORWITZ ELEMENTARY WAS **AWESOME**!

Herome Jorwitz Elementary
Best School in Quipa

Werica Ang

Hwo Beemuth

Choog

Kessy Drillman

THEY RESPECTED TEACHERS! THEY WERE ALWAYS ON TIME! THEY LOVED SCHOOL!

AT FIRST, THEY MISSED THEIR FRIENDS—LIKE GOOCH, ERICA, DRESSY, AND BO.

BUT THEN THEY DISCOVERED THAT THERE WERE A BUNCH OF STUDENTS WHO WERE EERILY SIMILAR TO THEM WHO WENT TO HEROME JORWITZ! THESE KIDS WERE THE SAME . . . BUT DIFFERENT.

So great to see you boys! I'm a new man, thanks to this amazing school!

SOON, THE BOYS REALIZED JUST HOW **BORING** EVERYTHING WAS. SO, THEY CREATED A COMIC TO SHOW THESE STRAIGHT-EDGED KIDS HOW TO LIVE A LITTLE.

You know what **I** just realized? Neamer's giant head makes him the bizarre version of Flabby Flab-ulous!

TO MAKE A LONG STORY SHORT: IT WORKED. BUT AFTER A PRANK-GONE-WRONG TURNED MR. MEANER'S OPPOSITE, MR. NEAMER, INTO BRAINY BLABULOUS, THEY HAD TO CALL ON CAPTAIN UNDERPANTS TO SAVE THE DAY.

(Remember Flabby Flab-ulous?)

TO BATTLE NEAMER'S MASSIVE BRAIN, CAPTAIN UNDERPANTS ENDED UP USING A LITTLE BRAWN . . . AND A LOT OF MINDLESS TV TO BREAK DOWN THOSE BRAIN CELLS.

CAPTAIN UNDERPANTS
AND the
CORRUPT CRUELIUS SNEEZER!

With Krupp and George and Harold back where they truly belonged, things could finally return to school-as-usual. Except, not quite. The fourth graders were preparing for a field trip to Romeinaday (Piqua's second-most-authentic ancient Rome reenactment experience). It sounded super-boring—so George and Harold decided to write a comic to figure out how they could spice up the trip in their own special way!

CHESAPEAKE MATH AND IT ELEMENT
6151 CHEVY CHASE DR
LAUREL MD 20707

November 13, 2019 at 7:42 AM

Sale Number	270
Register	500-004-973
Item Count	1
Transaction #	2767581930530255

ACU: TV PRANK POW..FICIAL GUIDEBOOK 9.99T

Tax Summary
  Sales Tax (6%)   0.60

Subtotal   9.99
Tax   0.60

Total   10.59
Cash   10.59

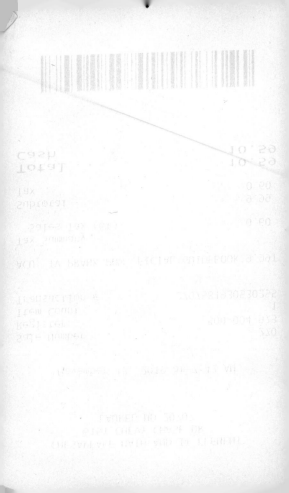

CAPTAIN UNDERPANTS
and the Crazy Caustic Spray of the Contagious Cruelius Sneezers

When George and Harold tricked Melvin into creating a time machine that could fit the *whole* class . . .

This is the TimeTanic 2000!

What have you rusty harmonicas done?

. . . their field trip to Romeinaday got much more interesting. Because instead of Romeinaday, they landed in **REAL** ancient Rome!

First, they had to battle the great and mighty (and undefeated) Undefeaticus in the gladiator arena.

Tra-La-Lion!

They survived that, but *then*, after reading George and Harold's latest comic book . . .

This comic feels pretty anti-me, but maybe that's just me.

. . . Julius Caesar fell into a bathtub filled with weird magic oils and turned into:

A GIANT NOSE!

CRUELIUS SNEEZER!

Luckily, this Emperor did *not* have a nose for roses . . .

Harold, fire up the rose-a-pult!

. . . so with the help of Captain Underpants and a bunch of sweet-smelling flowers . . .

. . . Cruelius Sneezer exploded in a mighty sneeze, launching the whole gang back to the TimeTanic 2000 (just in time to return home for afternoon dismissal)!

CAPTAIN UNDERPANTS
AND THE TUMULTUOUS
TUBBADUMP

WITH THE END OF THE SCHOOL YEAR APPROACHING, GEORGE AND HAROLD **REALLY** NEEDED TO STOP GETTING IN TROUBLE AND IMPROVE THEIR GRADES. OTHERWISE, THEY'D BE STUCK IN BORING OL' PIQUA ALL SUMMER, INSTEAD OF HAVING A BLAST AT LAKE SUMMER CAMP.

LUCKILY, A VERY LUCKY OPPORTUNITY CAME GEORGE AND HAROLD'S WAY. WHOEVER COULD FIGURE OUT THE BEST TRASH TRIBUTE FOR THE TOWN'S ANNUAL DUMP DAY—A MAJOR HOLIDAY THAT CELEBRATED PIQUA'S FOUNDER, HORATIO DUMP—WOULD EARN "ENOUGH EXTRA CREDIT TO CHOKE A HORSE." SO GEORGE AND HAROLD DECIDED TO FIRE UP THEIR IMAGINATIONS BY WRITING A COMIC.

I BE HORATIO DUMP'S GHOST! WHY ARE YE KICKIN' IT LIVE AT YON DUMP? TIS FOR TRASH, NOT PARTIES. WILL YE TAKE IT DOWN A NOTCH?

NO WAY, GRAMPS! IT'S DUMP DAY!

So, Ghost Dump raised his ghost arms and trash-piled onto him until he was a huge trash monster.

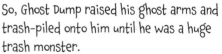

I'M TUBBADUMP AND YE WILL LEARN TO RESPECT THE TRASH!

Then Captain Underpants saw a teetering trash mountain behind Tubbadump and was all:

TRASH-ALANCHE! LADY-O LADY-O LADY-O HA-HEE!

Trash-alanche buried Tubbadump!

The ghost rose to attack again, but Captain Underpants bought him a fried gum on a stick and won him a fish.

And they became dump friends.

CAPTAIN UNDERPANTS
and the Trashy Tale of the Tumultuous Tubbadump

HORATIO DUMP
(portrayed here by a D-list actor in a low-budget reenactment)

THE ANNUAL PIQUA TRADITION OF HONORING HORATIO DUMP'S LEGACY BY TOSSING TRASH ALL OVER PIQUA TOOK A MESSY TURN . . .

. . . AFTER THE MELVINS DEVELOPED A DEVICE—THE SUCKOTRASH 2000—THAT COULD SUCK ALL THE GARBAGE OUT OF THE CITY. (MELVIN FELT IT WAS *ESSENTIAL* TO KEEP EVERYTHING AROUND THEIR SCHOOL CLEAN AND NEAT TO IMPRESS ELITEANATI ACADEMY.)

BUT AFTER CAPTAIN UNDERPANTS STOLE THE SUCKOTRASH 2000 . . .

GEORGE, HAROLD, AND THE CAPTAIN ACCIDENTALLY REVERSED THE DEVICE AND SENT ALL THE GARBAGE SPILLING BACK *INTO* THE CITY.

AND WITH THE TRASH, CAME *THIS* GUY:

ROAAAAAAAR!

THE REAL-LIFE TUBBADUMP TOOK A LOOK AT GEORGE AND HAROLD'S LATEST COMIC, AND DECIDED THEY HAD COME UP WITH SOME PRETTY GOOD IDEAS THAT HE COULD USE TO HIS ADVANTAGE.

SO, HE CREATED A GARBAGE AVALANCHE (JUST LIKE THE TRASHALANCHE IN GEORGE AND HAROLD'S COMIC)!

I will destroy your entire dimension! This mess is gonna mess you up!

LUCKILY, THANKS TO SOME QUICK THINKING, AN ASSIST FROM CAPTAIN UNDERPANTS, AND A WELL-TIMED GOLDEN DUMPY AWARD, GEORGE AND HAROLD SAVED THE DAY *AND* EARNED A MASSIVE PILE OF EXTRA CREDIT . . . WHICH SHOT THEM STRAIGHT TO THE TOP OF THE RANK TANK 2000!

RANK TANK 2000

GEORGE
HAROLD

MELVIN
ERICA

EMILY

BUT BEFORE THEY COULD PACK UP AND HEAD OFF TO LAKE SUMMER CAMP, GEORGE AND HAROLD HAD TO KEEP THEIR GRADES ABOVE THE PASSING LINE FOR THE LAST FEW WEEKS OF SCHOOL . . .

CAPTAIN UNDERPANTS

and the

DEADLY DOOM DOME

With the school year almost over, George and Harold were feeling confident. There was **NOTHING** that could knock them far enough down on Melvin's Rank Tank 2000 to ruin camp for them. Or **WAS** there? What if one of their own **COMICS** was responsible for their downfall?!

One time, Captain Underpants went to the mall to get the new Punt Force Mama album.

Then this cool dude with a sweet mustache was all:

WANNA GO TO THE PUNT FORCE MAMA CONCERT? THEY GIVE OUT FREE TICKETS AT THE OIL-CHANGE PLACE.

TRA-LA-LAY IT ON ME!

So, they went to the new ThisIsn'tATrap Dome (which didn't sound suspicious at all).

This isn't a TRAP DOME

NO! HE HAS THE VOICE OF AN ANGEL—WITH A SORE THROAT!

So, Captain Underpants chased them . . .

. . . but Dr. Disgruntled set a bunch of traps!

Like a man-eating plant, called Meanus Guy Trap.

The Sproing in Your Steps

The Stupefying Stairs of Stink

Fingers, the Petty Thief Panther

And Drowsy Darts that used band merch as bait.

But Captain Underpants brought his U-game, cuz UNDERWEAR! And he beat the traps cuz that's what heroes do.

CAPTAIN UNDERPANTS
and the Taxing Trauma of the Treacherous Tattle Trials

With George and Harold ending the year as the top students at Melvin Sneedly Elementary, Melvin's dream of attending Eliteanati Academy had turned into just that: a dream. Eliteanati would only accept a school's top student, and that was *NOT* Melvin anymore. **UNLESS:** Melvin and Principal Melvinborg could come up with an idea so **BIG** that it would knock George and Harold right out of the game. Then Melvin would be number one again, and all his dreams would come true.

RELAX. THERE ARE STILL FIVE DAYS OF SCHOOL LEFT, AND I HAVE A PLAN. I'VE DEVISED A FINAL EXAM FOR YOUR CLASS, RIGGED SO YOU CAN RECLAIM THE TOP SPOT AND GET THAT INVITATION FROM ELITEANATI. I'M CALLING IT THE TATTLE TRIALS.

GEORGE AND HAROLD SURVIVED *THAT*. BUT THEN, AFTER THEY STOLE MELVIN'S PHONE AND TURNED UP ALL THE NANOBOTS INSIDE MELVIN'S BODY . . .

. . . THEY HAD A MUCH **BIGGER** PROBLEM TO DEAL WITH.

TIME TO CALL ON CAPTAIN UNDERPANTS FOR HELP!

Ugh. Drowsy Darts! What were we thinking when we put that in our comic?

UH-OH. SO MUCH FOR HELP FROM THE CAPTAIN.

And **THAT'S** when things went from bad . . . to worse . . . to much *much* worse. When he was trying to shrink Melvin back down to normal size, Melvinborg accidentally transferred the nanobots that had been inside Melvin's body into the *dome*.

Suddenly, these five found themselves trapped inside an evil dome. Now there were even more obstacles to overcome in order to pass their final exam . . . and survive fourth grade!

WE HAVE TO GET TO THE DOME'S EMERGENCY SHUTDOWN SWITCH.

First came the Uncontrolli-bulls 2000.

THEY *FINALLY* REACHED THE PIT FULL OF ELECTRIC LAVA THAT HOUSED THE DOME'S EMERGENCY SHUTDOWN SWITCH. CAPTAIN UNDERPANTS DOVE IN AND FOUND THE SWITCH. TIME FOR A HAPPY ENDING?

NOPE.

Is anybody else's head buzzing? Like a bunch of little robots are trying to take over your brain?

UH-OH. SHUTTING DOWN THE DOME FORCED THE NANOBOTS TO FIND A NEW HOST.

CAPTAIN UNDERPANTS GREW AND GREW AND GREW UNTIL HE WAS **GIANT.** AND THEN ... HE TURNED INTO EVIL **CAPTAIN NANOPANTS**!

For too long, bigs have oppressed smalls. Now we small nanobots have the means to reap vengeance. Phase One is your obliteration!

CAPTAIN UNDERPANTS AND THE NIGHTMARISH NANO ZERO

With Captain Nanopants on a rampage and Melvin unsure of how to fix this **MASSIVE** problem, George and Harold decided it was time for them to take control of the situation. What's the best way to solve every problem? Write a comic!

So, there was a bad nanobot named Nanozero who was tiny. Like, dollhouse furniture tiny times a quillion.

He was the boss of a nanobot gang destroying stuff like taco trucks . . .

. . . and horse spas. Everybody was all, "Did a ghost break that?" Cuz they couldn't see the nanobots and ghosts are a menace.

But then Nanozero's gang snuck into the President of Earth's brain . . .

and took it over.

WHO NEEDS DOCTORS?

I'M CANCELING THE SPACE PROGRAM!

BIG IS BAD!

So, the Vice President of Earth activated the Captain Underpants signal.

THE TATTLE TRIALS:
PART 2

Using their latest comic as a guide, George and Harold came up with a plan of attack. As Captain Nanopants continued his rampage through Piqua . . .

George, Harold, and Melvin hopped into a handy hovercraft (made out of half of Melvinborg's body!) . . .

156

. . . AND SHRUNK THEMSELVES DOWN USING MELVIN'S YOUWANTSIZEWITHTHAT 2000.

THEN THEY BLASTED INSIDE CAPTAIN UNDERPANTS'S BRAIN, WHICH LOOKED JUST LIKE GEORGE AND HAROLD HAD ALWAYS IMAGINED IT WOULD LOOK.

TRA-LA-LAAAAAND!

Everybody here is filled with glee! Cuz everywhere you look it's me, me, me!

THEY HAD TO GET PAST THE BRAIN CELLS THAT HAD ALREADY BEEN CORRUPTED BY NANOBOTS AND TAKE NANOZERO DOWN! (BEFORE CAPTAIN UNDERPANTS WAS LOST TO EVIL FOREVER.)

Using the annoying song they'd heard playing inside Captain Underpants's own brain as a weapon, George and Harold hoped to destroy Nanozero the same way it had been done in their comic. To make a long story short: it worked.

Then Melvin made a big move of his own . . .

NOW LET'S LEAVE GEORGE AND HAROLD HERE, TRAPPED FOREVER IN NANOZERO'S HUSK. MWA-HA-HA!

I refuse to become the monster you are when I grow up. And that decision means you no longer exist!

All's well that ends well . . . or is it?

There was just one thing left to do: Melvin had to return to the Doom Dome and push the big red button so he could win the Tattle Trials and reclaim his spot as top student. But before he could push the button, **ERICA** swooped in and beat him to it. Now *she* would get Melvin's invite to Eliteanati Academy!

So, yeah, things didn't end quite as they were supposed to. Even though Krupp regained his title as principal . . .

HOPE DIES HERE

. . . poor Melvin could now officially kiss Eliteanati goodbye. As for George and Harold? In an extreme case of bad luck (and clever plotting), George and Harold found out they'd been placed in two *different* summer camps.

UH-OH. That can't be good.

Camp Lake Summer Camp?

Lake Summer Camp Camp?

SUMMER CAMP BATTLE-O-RAMA

School was finally out for summer and _____ was excited to go to Camp
(your first name)

_____!
(name of summer camp)

But when the camp counselors showed up, they both looked very familiar. These

weren't regular camp counselors. They were characters _____ and
(your first name)

_____ had made a comic about during a boring _____ class! One of
(your friend's name)   (school subject)

the counselors had oozing _____ skin and giant _____ for arms. The
(color)   (kitchen utensil, plural)

other had a giant _____ where his head should be!
(body part)

"Hey!" shouted _____. "You're not camp counselors! You're _____
(your first name)   (same color)

_____ Hands and _____ _____ Head!
(same kitchen utensil as above)   (gross adjective)   (same body part as above)

_____ and I created you!"
(same friend's name)

"Mwa-ha-ha!" the evil counselors laughed. "You're right! And now we are here to

make this summer _____. Nothing can stop us!"
(adjective)

"Captain Underpants can!" cried _____.
(your first name)

"Tra-La-Laaaaa!" yelled Captain Underpants as he _____ into the woods.
(verb ending in -ed)

"I am here to save the camp." He grabbed a _____ and whipped it at
(large thing found in the woods)

the _____ counselors. Both of the evil counselors flew up into the air and
(evil adjective)

_____ into the lake!
(verb ending in -ed)

"Yay!" shouted all the campers. "_____ and Captain Underpants saved
(your first name)

summer camp! Let's all eat _____ and go _____."
(yummy summer food, plural)   (summer-y verb ending in -ing.)

Reminder:
A **VERB** is an action word (like *run, hop, smash, crush,* etc.)
An **ADJECTIVE** is a word that describes a person, place, or thing (like *stinky, green, slimy, gross,* etc.)